DEMON SLAYER

THE CROW

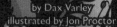

by Dax Varley
illustrated by Jon Proctor

Spellbound

An Imprint of Magic Wagon
abdopublishing.com

*Huge thanks to Julie Pitzel, Bob Mann, Vicki Sansum, and
Lenny Enderle. —DV*

For Glenn —JP

abdopublishing.com

Printed in the United States of America, North Mankato, Minnesota.
052016
092016

♻ THIS BOOK CONTAINS
RECYCLED MATERIALS

Written by Dax Varley
Illustrated by Jon Proctor
Edited by Tamara L. Britton and Megan M. Gunderson
Designed by Candice Keimig

Cataloging-in-Publication Data

Names: Varley, Dax, author. | Proctor, Jon, illustrator.
Title: The crow / by Dax Varley ; illustrated by Jon Proctor.
Description: Minneapolis, MN : Magic Wagon, [2017] | Series: Demon
    slayer ; #4
Summary: Max may have finally found his mom with the help of a very
    smart crow, but finding her is just the beginning.
Identifiers: LCCN 2016934393 | ISBN 9781624021602 (lib. bdg.) |
    ISBN 9781680790108 (ebook)
Subjects: LCSH: Mothers and sons--Fiction. | Kidnapping--Fiction. |
    Demonology--Fiction.
Classification: DDC [Fic]--dc23
LC record available at http://lccn.loc.gov/2016934393

TABLE OF
CONTENTS

CHAPTER 1
CAW, CAW! 4

CHAPTER 2
MOM! 16

CHAPTER 3
EMPTY AGONY 26

CHAPTER 4
HELLO, POE 44

CAW, CAW!

The bread in my hideout had molded. The **RATS** didn't care. I tossed them large chunks so they'd leave me alone. I had work to do. I *double-checked* my supplies.

4

Two extra elastic bands for my
SLINGSHOT.
Three large bottles of *witch hazel.*

Sixty-four game tokens.

I'd never run out of tokens.

As ammo, they make demons go **POP!** Then I simply pick up the tokens off the ground and reuse them.

At dusk, I went to the cemetery and climbed my favorite tree. I didn't have to wait long. Soon, a dozen of them gathered to eat the dirt. I readied my weapon, pulled it tight, and—*CAW!* A stupid crow landed, scaring the bejeebers out of me.

CAW!

"Shoo," I whispered.

CAW! CAW!

9

Wait . . . demons can shape-shift.
I checked its **beady** eyes. It
tilted its head, checking me out too.
I misted it with witch hazel. "Shoo."

The crow ruffled its feathers, shaking the branch.

The demons froze and looked up. "It's him!" one hissed.

They scattered.

CAW!

"You warned them." I turned my weapon on the bird.

"Ouch!" It **PECKED** my hand. Jerking back, I dropped the slingshot. The crow swooped, pecked it up, and flew high.

"No!" I plunged to the ground and ran after the bird.

It flew slowly, always in sight.

Twice I threw tokens at it. **Stupid**, I know. But dang it, I wanted my slingshot back.

As we got deeper into the woods, the crow perched on a branch. I rushed forward and, "What the . . ." I'd stepped into a **SINKHOLE**.

"Help!" I hollered,
like anyone other than
the crow would hear
me. **QUICKSAND!** That
idiot crow had led me
to the Wailing Woods.

CAW!

CHAPTER 2

MOM!

I grabbed at the marshy grass,
but it bent and sank with me.

Down.

Down.

Down.

"Help!"

With one huge *sluuurrrp*,
the earth sucked me under.

I held my breath, sinking deeper and deeper. Mud OOZED into my nostrils. My lungs burned for air. Then, suddenly, I fell—landing hard.

I sucked air through my mouth, wiped gook from my eyes, and blew it from my nose. GROANING, I pulled myself up. Had I cracked a rib? Better than drowning in quicksand.

I was in a pit of some sort. A blue light **SHONE** in. Could that be a way out? I hurried toward it, turned a corner, and before me stood a clear glass wall. Behind it, floating in a pool of neon fluid, were a dozen *redheaded* women. All sleeping.

I spotted Abby Davis, a classmate who'd vanished a month before. Then I saw *her*. "Mom!"

I raced over and beat on the glass. "Mom! ***MOM!***"

She continued to **FLOAT**, face up. Her hair long and billowing like Rapunzel's. I kicked the glass, over and over. Too thick. I wasn't even sure it was glass. "Mom!"

One woman floated in front of me. I'd seen her picture in the paper after she'd disappeared. Her *buzz cut* hair prickled from her head. Then I noticed, Abby's was shorter too. A few of them had hair longer than Mom's. *What's the deal?*

I kicked the glass a few more times. Useless. *Get help,* I told myself.

I went back to where I'd fallen and looked around. A tree root jutted through the dirt. I clamped on and **climbed**.

When I neared the top, I pulled my shirt up over my face. Then, holding my breath, pushed upward through the **sludge**.

I soon felt the air above ground, but this time it came with a familiar stink. I popped my head out of my shirt. That's when four claws RAKED my jaw.

CHAPTER 3

EMPTY AGONY

"Ahhh!" I pulled myself from the gunk. I got up on my hands and knees and pounded my **sunburst** ring into the demon's foot.

One down, but two more charged. I stood up just as one nasty **DEVIL** pounced. I drew up my knees and cannonballed him.

I stood, holding up my **FISTS**.

"That's right. Come get me."

That's when another demon crept up behind me. He grabbed my arms, PINNING them.

Using a smelly rag, another demon twisted the ring off my finger. I got my arm free. But I couldn't stop the demon from throwing my ring into the woods.

The demon turned to me. "We've had enough of you, Max."

"What are you doing to my mother? And Abby? And the other **redheads**?"

"We need them," he said. "Darkness comes, and you can thank your mom for that." His mouth peaked into a **HIDEOUS** grin. "Oh wait. You can't. You'll be dead." He laughed in my face.

I raised my feet and kicked, knocking him to the ground. But the one behind me sank his **TEETH** into my neck.

My **SCREAMS** bounced through the woods. Hot  rolled down my back. Stars burst before my eyes.

I'm going to die.

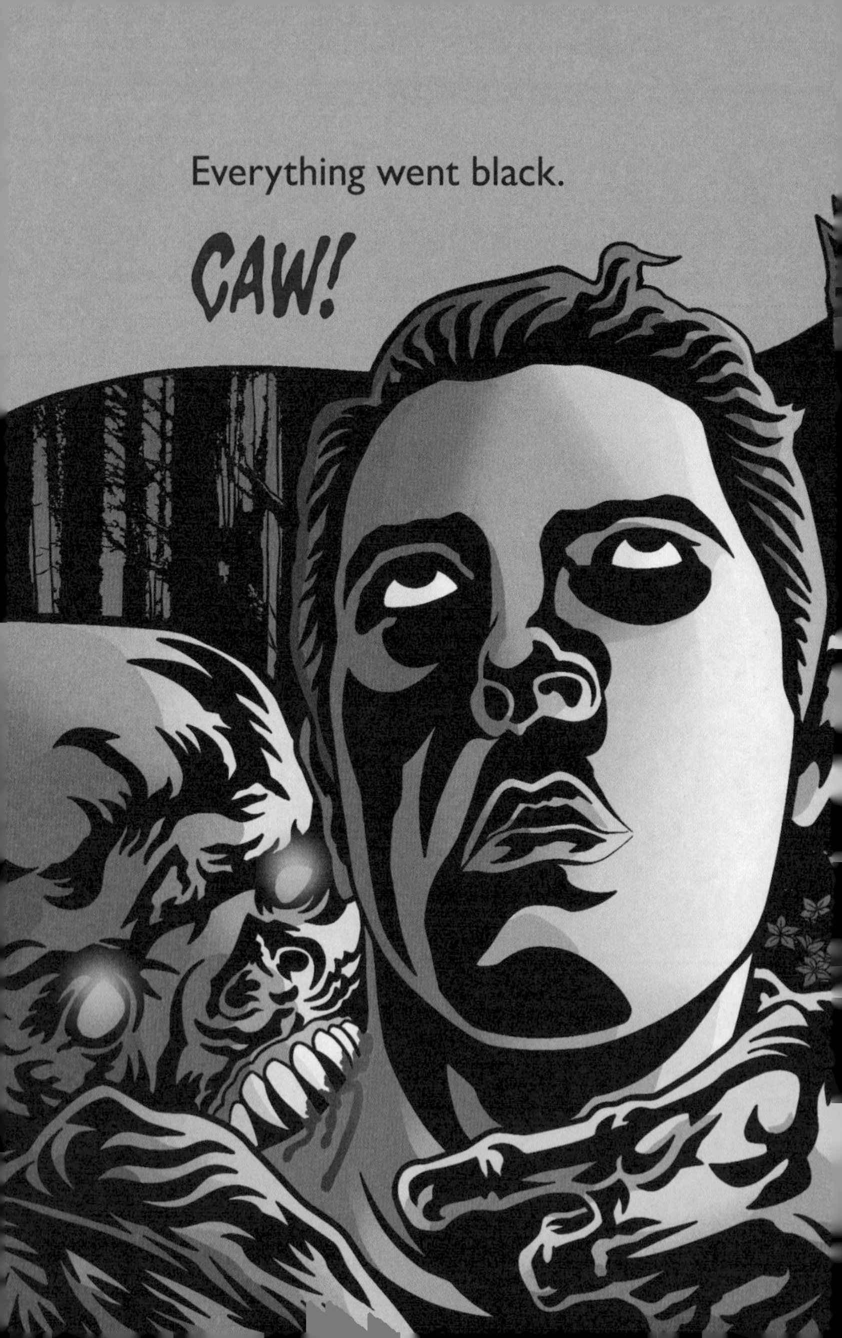
Everything went black.
CAW!

My eyes *fluttered* open, bleary. It felt like someone had parked a Volkswagen on my ribs. My neck **BURNED** from the bite. How long had I been out?

I managed to stand. *Whoa!* Three demons lay dead around me, their eyes missing, their bodies PECKED full of HOLES. And that wasn't all. My slingshot!

I glanced down at the hole in the ground. *Mom!* I quickly called Dad's phone. It went to voice mail. I'd forgotten he was at a support group with the families of the missing redheads. I smiled to myself. Would I have a surprise for them.

I raced home. After cleaning up my **NASTY** wounds, I gathered my ammo, and covered myself head to foot in *witch hazel*. Grabbing a shovel and rope, I went back to the Wailing Woods.

I dug, making the hole bigger,
then climbed in. Complete
DARKNESS. *Where was the blue light?*

I clicked on my flashlight app and flew around the corner. The glass wall was still there. But behind it? Nothing. Drained.

"Ahhh!" My screams of **agony** echoed through the cavern. *Where had they taken Mom?* I fell to my knees.

CHAPTER 4

HELLO, POE

Once home, I fell onto my bed, holding back **tears**. *So close. So close. So close.*

Something tapped on my WINDOWPANE, causing me to jump. The crow.

I opened the window. Had this bird really taken out three *DEMONS* on its own? That's when I noticed something in its mouth. My ring. The crow dropped it onto the sill.

"Want to come in?" I asked.

The bird winged past me and perched on my bookshelf.

"Thanks for *saving* me."

I dug a half-empty pack of sunflower seeds from my desk. "I'm going to call you **POE** after the guy who wrote 'The Raven.'"

It tilted its head, as in thought.

Then spreading out some seeds,
I said, "You found my mother once,
you can do it again, right? We could
do it **TOGETHER**."
Poe fluttered his wings. *CAW!*